Where do dinosaurs shop?

What did the Triceratops land on when he fell down?

STEGOSAURUS

How do you know a dinosaur is asleep?

What do you do if you find a dinosaur sleeping in your bed?

What does a dinosaur say right before bed?

Why did the dinosaur eat so fast?

What is a dinosaur's favorite kind of party?

How can you tell if a dinosaur has been in your refrigerator?

What kind of
stories do
dinosaurs
like?

What kind
of dinosaur
has a messy
room?

Why
did the
dinosaur
love his
cat?

What do you call
a dinosaur bike?

Why did the
dinosaur kick
the soccer ball?

Why did the dinosaur's school bus stop?

TSINTAOSAURUS

Why did the dinosaur take a bath?

How can you tell if a dinosaur took a bath?

When a dinosaur splashes water out of the tub, where does it go?

What did the dinosaur do at the playground?

Why did the dinosaur cross the monkey bars?

What do you sa

hen you slide down a dinosaur's neck?

So dinosaur jokes make a dinosaur laugh.
I hope you have giggled on dino's behalf.
With a dinosaur chortle,
a snort and hee-haw,
a cackle and snicker,
a silly guffaw,
we'll leave you to
share one dino
joke more.